I'm Big Enough

Sally Odgers illustrated by Lloyd Foye

Flying Frog Publishing

For Kerrin, Kiarna and Katelyn-S.O.
For J and J-L.F.

Joey was hopping along with his mother.

Hoppity-hop went Mom.
Hoppity-hoppity-hop went Joey.

"Mom," said Joey, "I'm getting big now.
May I hop alone?"

"You could ride in my pouch if you can't keep up,"
said Mom.

"No," said Joey. "I'm big enough to hop alone.
You hop ahead and wait at Wallaby Grove."

"Do you know the way?" asked Mom.

"Yes," said Joey. "Past Pretty Creek, Big Rock, Great Gum, Wattle Knob, and then it's **Wallaby Grove**."

"Fine," said Mom. "Hop along then. You can hop on your own."

"I know I can," said Joey.

He stretched up high and kissed his mother's nose. "I'll see you when I get to **Wallaby Grove**."

Joey nibbled grass, but the land seemed wide
and suddenly much too quiet.
I'd better hop along now, thought Joey.

Hoppity-hoppity-hop,
he hopped toward Pretty Creek.

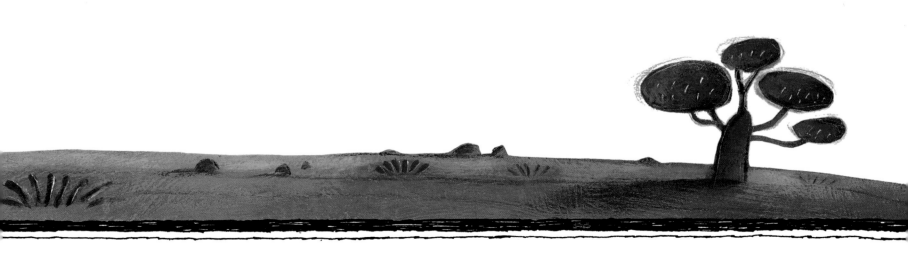

"Hello, Joey," said Platypus. "What are you doing all alone?"

"I'm hopping to Wallaby Grove," said Joey proudly.

"Ridiculous!" said Platypus. "You're too little."

Joey Hopalong was disappointed. "I'm big enough to hop alone," he said.

"Oh!" said Platypus. "Prove it. Try to catch a juicy worm."

"Ugh!" said Joey. "I can't catch a worm."

Platypus climbed up the bank.

"I didn't think so," he said. "That just shows you're too little to hop alone, so I'll come, too."

Hoppity-hoppity-hop,

Joey hopped toward Big Rock.
Platypus ran along beside him.

"Hello," said Wombat. "Where is Joey going?"

"He's off to Wallaby Grove," said Platypus.

"Really?" said Wombat. "He's too *little*."

Joey Hopalong was disappointed.
"I'm big enough to hop alone," he said.

"All right," said Wombat. "Prove it. Try to dig a nifty burrow."

Joey scraped with his claws,
but he couldn't dig a burrow.

"You do it like this," said Wombat,
and she dug a nifty burrow.

"That settles it. I'm coming along.
You're too little to hop alone."

Hoppity-hoppity-hop,
Joey hopped toward Great Gum.
Platypus ran and Wombat shuffled along.

"What a terribly long way," said Wombat,
"for someone so *little*."

Maybe they're right, thought Joey.
I couldn't catch a worm or dig a burrow.

Hoppity-hoppity-hop.

Joey hopped under Great Gum.

"Joey Hopalong!" said Possum. "What are you doing here without your mother?"

"He's off to Wallaby Grove," said Wombat.

"He's too little to hop alone," said Platypus.

"I thought I was big enough," said Joey sadly, "but I can't catch a worm or dig a burrow."

"All right," said Possum. "Hang by your tail.
That will prove you're not too little."

Joey looked at Great Gum,
then peered back at his tail.
"I can't do that," he said.
"My tail doesn't bend enough!"

"See?" said Possum.
"You're too little to hop alone."

Joey Hopalong was disappointed.

"Never mind," said Wombat.
"We'll look after you."

Hoppity-hoppity-hop.

Joey hopped toward Wattle Knob. Platypus ran,
Wombat shuffled, and Possum scurried beside him.

"Hello, Joey Hopalong," called Kookaburra.
"Where are you going with such a mob?"

"To Wallaby Grove," said Joey.

"He's only little," Platypus said, "he can't even catch a worm!"

"Right," said Wombat. "He's too little to dig a burrow."

"He's too *little* to hang by his tail!" said Possum.

"And he thought he was big
enough to hop alone!"

Kookaburra laughed
and flapped her wings.

"Let's see him fly!" she said.
"That will prove he's not too little."

Everybody stared at Kookaburra.

"But—" said Wombat.

"But—" said Possum.

"But—" said Platypus.

"How could he do that?"

"Come on," said Kookaburra.
"Show us how you fly!"

"I haven't got any wings!" said Joey. "How could I fly? I'm not a Kookaburra!"

"Right," said Kookaburra.

"Hey!" said Platypus. "We never thought of that."

"No," said Wombat and Possum. "All the same, he's only little."

"What can you do?" Kookaburra asked Joey.
"Can you prove you're big enough to hop alone?"

"I hop along," said Joey.
"That's what kangaroos do when they're getting big."

"Hop along, then," said Kookabura.

So Joey hopped along.

Joey hopped to **Wallaby Grove.**

"Hey, Mom," said Joey.
 "Kangaroos can't catch worms!
They can't dig burrows, or hang by their tails.
 And they sure can't fly."

"Right!" said Mom.
 "And why would they
 want to?"

"Beats me," said Joey,
and kissed his mother's nose.